Katie Kazoo, SWITCHEROO

Hair Today, Gone Tomorrow!

by Nancy Krulik • illustrated by John & Wendy

Grosset & Dunlap
An Imprint of Penguin Group (USA) Inc.

For Amanda, who has her own sense of sparkle, and for Ian, our resident musician. Thanks for helping me keep it real.—N.K.

For the ultra-fabulous Miss Mary Jones.—J&W

GROSSET & DUNLAP
Published by the Penguin Group
Penguin Group (USA) Inc., 375 Hudson Street, New York,
New York 10014, USA
Penguin Group (Canada), 90 Eglinton Avenue East, Suite 700, Toronto,
Ontario M4P 2Y3, Canada
(a division of Pearson Penguin Canada Inc.)
Penguin Books Ltd., 80 Strand, London WC2R 0RL, England
Penguin Group Ireland, 25 St. Stephen's Green, Dublin 2,
Ireland(a division of Penguin Books Ltd.)
Penguin Group (Australia), 250 Camberwell Road, Camberwell, Victoria 3124,
Australia(a division of Pearson Australia Group Pty. Ltd.)
Penguin Books India Pvt. Ltd., 11 Community Centre, Panchsheel Park,
New Delhi—110 017, India
Penguin Group (NZ), 67 Apollo Drive, Rosedale, North Shore 0632,
New Zealand (a division of Pearson New Zealand Ltd.)
Penguin Books (South Africa) (Pty.) Ltd., 24 Sturdee Avenue,
Rosebank, Johannesburg 2196, South Africa

Penguin Books Ltd., Registered Offices:
80 Strand, London WC2R 0RL, England

Library of Congress Control Number: 2009027498

ISBN 978-0-448-45231-9   10 9 8 7 6 5 4 3 2 1

Chapter 1

Camptown ladies sing this song. Doo-dah. Doo-dah.

The Camptown racetrack's five miles long. Oh, the doo-dah day!

Katie Carew rocked back and forth happily as she played the familiar song on her clarinet.

"Great job!" Mr. Starkey, the school music teacher, told the beginning band. "You guys really sound terrific."

Katie smiled. For a long time, everything the band played had sounded like a bunch of squeaks and squawks.

"In fact," Mr. Starkey continued, "you guys are *so* great, it's time you gave a concert."

"Wow! For real?" Jeremy Fox exclaimed from behind his drum set. He hit his cymbal to celebrate.

"Where?" Becky Stern asked.

"In the auditorium," Mr. Starkey told her. "Next Monday night."

Katie gulped. Monday night was just a week away. Would they be ready for a concert by then?

"What are we going to play?" she asked Mr. Starkey nervously.

"'Camptown Races' will be ready," Mr. Starkey told her. "You guys also sound great on 'Go Tell Aunt Rhodie' and 'Hot Cross Buns.'"

"Three songs?" Kevin Camilleri asked. "That's not a very long concert."

"True," Mr. Starkey said. "But the beginning band won't be the only group playing at this concert. The fifth-grade band will be playing, too."

"The fifth-grade band is awesome," George Brennan pointed out. "We'll never sound nearly as good as them."

Mr. Starkey nodded. "That's why we're going to have extra rehearsals during recess this week," he said. "Okay?"

Katie wasn't sure how she felt about that. She really loved recess time. So did all her friends. But everybody in the band—Katie included—also loved playing music.

The kids looked around at one another and shrugged. "Okay," they all agreed.

"Great," Mr. Starkey said with a smile. "Let's try 'Camptown Races' again." He lifted his arms. The kids picked up their instruments and began to play.

Camptown ladies sing this song. Doo-dah. Doo-dah.

The Camptown racetrack's five miles long. Oh, the doo-dah day!

Chapter 2

Katie couldn't wait to tell her mom about
the concert. She ran all the way home—which
wasn't easy, since she was carrying her clarinet
case and her backpack.

"Mom!" Katie shouted as she raced into her
house.

"Ruff! Ruff!" Katie's chocolate and white
cocker spaniel, Pepper, jumped at her heels.
He could tell something really exciting had
happened.

"What is it?" Mrs. Carew asked as she came
from the kitchen.

"I'm going to play the clarinet in a concert,"
Katie exclaimed.

"That *is* great news!" Mrs. Carew agreed.

"The concert's at school," Katie continued. "In the auditorium. Everyone's invited."

"Ruff! Ruff!" Pepper barked happily.

Katie bent down and scratched Pepper behind one of his long, fluffy ears. "Well, almost everyone," she told him. "Dogs aren't allowed in school."

Pepper wagged his tail, anyway. He loved being scratched behind the ears.

"When is the concert?" Katie's mom asked.

"Next Monday," Katie replied.

Katie's mother wasn't smiling quite so widely now.

"What's the matter?" Katie asked.

"Well, I can be at the concert," Katie's mom said. "But Daddy called a little while ago. He's leaving town on business."

"But I want him to hear me play," she insisted.

"I understand," Katie's mom said. "But he can't get out of this trip. I'll tell you what. I'll bring the video camera and tape the concert."

"That's not the same!" Katie exclaimed. "I . . ."

Katie stopped before she could say another word. She had been about to wish her dad didn't have to go on business trips. But Katie knew wishes could bring trouble. Especially when they came true.

It had all started one horrible day back in third grade. First, Katie had missed the football and lost the game for her team. Then she'd fallen in the mud and ruined her new jeans. Worst of all, she'd let out a giant burp right in front of the whole class.

It had definitely been one of the most embarrassing days of Katie's whole life. And that night, Katie wished she could be anyone but herself. There must have been a shooting star flying overhead when Katie made her wish, because the very next day the magic wind came.

The magic wind was unlike any wind Katie had ever seen before. It was a wild, fierce tornado that only blew around Katie.

But the worst part came after the wind *stopped* blowing. That meant Katie had turned into someone else. One . . . two . . . switcheroo!

The first time the magic wind appeared, it changed her into Speedy, the hamster in her third-grade classroom. Katie spent the whole morning going around and around on a hamster wheel and chewing on Speedy's wooden chew sticks. *Blech!*

The magic wind came back over and over again after that. Once the magic wind had even turned Katie into Mr. Starkey. Katie didn't know a thing about being a music teacher. She'd tried to conduct the beginning band—the very same band she was in. It sounded awful. No. Make that *worse* than awful. The band sounded so bad that all the kids had wanted to quit playing music. That just couldn't happen again, not when everyone was so excited about the concert.

That was why Katie didn't make wishes anymore. Wishes caused too much trouble. Still, it would have been nice if her dad could have been at the concert.

"Why don't you invite some of your friends to come hear you play?" Katie's mom suggested.

"All my friends are in the band," Katie said. "They'll be onstage with me."

"Suzanne doesn't play an instrument," her mom reminded her. "And I'll bet she'd love to come."

Katie brightened a little. It would be nice to have her best friend hear her play in the concert.

"Okay," Katie said. "I'll call her right now."

As Katie walked to the phone, she crossed her fingers, hoping Suzanne would say yes. Hoping was different than wishing. Hoping never caused Katie any trouble at all.

Chapter 3

"Oh, Katie, that's so cool!" Suzanne said when Katie called her. "You've never been in a concert before, have you?"

"No," Katie replied.

"In fact, you've never been onstage before," Suzanne continued.

Katie sighed. That wasn't completely true. Katie *had* been onstage. It happened when the magic wind

came and switcherooed her into Suzanne just
before a modeling show.

And then there was the time when the whole
fourth grade was waiting to see a Presidents'
Day show at the Cherrydale Arena. Katie
had suddenly found herself onstage—playing
President Millard Fillmore of all people!

But Suzanne didn't know anything about
Katie's "performances."

"So what are you going to wear onstage?"
Suzanne asked Katie.

"I don't know," Katie replied. "I don't think it
matters."

"*Of course* it matters,"
Suzanne insisted. "You
have to look great. That
way the audience will
focus on you."

"But—" Katie began.

Suzanne didn't let Katie finish the sentence. "My modeling class has a runway show on Saturday afternoon," she continued. "And I'm already thinking about what I'm going to wear and how I'm going to do my hair."

"The audience is supposed to focus on the music," Katie reminded Suzanne. "A music recital is different than a modeling recital."

"First of all, it's not called a modeling recital. It's a *runway show*," Suzanne told Katie. "And second of all, it's not that different. You're performing, so you have to look good."

"I guess," Katie said slowly. "I never thought of it that way."

"Of course you didn't," Suzanne said. "But that's what you have me for. I'm going to that new hair salon in the mall on Saturday morning. You should come with me. We can both have our hair done."

"What new hair salon?" Katie asked.

"It's called Sparkle's Salon," Suzanne told

her. She sounded very happy to know something Katie didn't. "It's right next to the flower shop."

"Well, if you really think I need a haircut . . ." Katie said hesitantly.

"Not just a cut," Suzanne said. "You need a whole new style."

That made Katie feel bad. "What's wrong with my old style?" she asked.

"Nothing," Suzanne said, trying to sound a little nicer. "It's just that I thought a change might be good."

"Well, maybe," Katie began. "But I don't know if—"

"Don't worry about a thing," Suzanne continued. "I'll make sure Sparkle gives you a gorgeous cut. I'll take care of everything."

But Katie *was* worried. With Suzanne in charge, there was no telling what could happen.

Chapter 4

The next morning, Katie walked into her classroom. Hair was the last thing on her mind. Then she took a look at Mr. G.

Whoa! Her teacher was wearing a bald cap over *his* hair. He was also wearing knickers and holding a kite with a key on the end.

It was a very strange outfit. Even for Mr. Guthrie.

"Good morning, Katie Kazoo." Mr. G. greeted Katie, using the way-cool nickname George had given her last year.

"Good morning, Mr. . . . um . . . uh?" Katie wasn't sure what to call him. Mr. G. often dressed up in costumes. And usually Katie knew who he was supposed to be. But not today.

"Don't you recognize me?" Mr. G. asked Katie.

Katie shook her head.

"He's Benjamin Franklin," George called out.

"How could you tell?" Katie asked.

"It's the kite," George explained. "Benjamin

Franklin used a kite with a key on the end when he did his experiments with electricity."

"How did you know *that*?" Kevin asked George.

"I used to live near Philadelphia," George explained. "They're crazy about Benjamin Franklin in Philadelphia. He lived there."

That made sense to Katie. George's family had moved around a lot. George had lived in a lot of places, so he knew a lot of interesting facts the rest of the kids didn't.

"Are we learning about Philadelphia now?" Katie asked.

"Nope," Mr. G. told her. "Guess again."

Katie looked around the classroom for a hint as to what their next learning adventure could be. It didn't take long to figure it out. There were diamond-shaped kites taped to the wall. Two big, colorful, box-shaped kites were hanging from the ceiling. And in the corner was a long, yellow, pink, and green, snake-shaped kite. It was hanging right over Slinky's cage.

Which made sense, since Slinky was their class snake.

"We're learning about kites!" Katie declared excitedly.

"Exactly," Mr. G. told her.

"How much can there be to learn about kites?" Andrew Epstein asked Mr. G. "You build them, you fly them, then you watch them crash on the ground."

"There's a lot to know about kites," Mr. G. assured Andrew. "Like, for instance, did you ever wonder why kites can fly even though they are actually heavier than air?"

"How do they do that?" Katie asked her teacher.

"That's for you to find out," Mr. G. told her. "You can start when we go to the library later this morning."

"There are *whole books* written about kites?" Andrew asked.

Mr. G. nodded. "Kites are really interesting," he said. "You'll be surprised at what you'll learn."

Katie smiled. That was what she liked most about being in Mr. G.'s class. With a teacher who dressed up like Ben Franklin and hung giant kites from the ceiling, *every day* was full of surprises.

Chapter 5

At lunch later that day, everyone in the fourth grade was talking about kites. Class 4B was studying them, too. But their teacher, Ms. Sweet, hadn't dressed up like Benjamin Franklin. Only Mr. G. would do something like that.

"Ms. Sweet told us about the very first kite," Jeremy said to Katie, Emma W., Kevin, and George. "About two thousand years ago, a Chinese farmer tied a string to his hat to keep it from blowing away in the wind."

"That's a cool story," Katie told him. "Do you know if it's true?"

Jeremy shrugged. "I don't know. It could be."

"Well, I know something that *is* true," Kevin

said. "Kites are named for the kite bird. That's a member of the hawk family."

"Mr. G. taught us that," George added.

"Well, Ms. Sweet told *us* that kites were used during the Civil War to deliver letters and newspapers," Manny Gonzalez said.

"Kites are heavier than air," Katie told the kids. "But they fly because the force of the wind pressure on the kite gives it lift. I read that in a book in the library."

"Impressive," Jeremy complimented her.

"And I learned that the longest kite fly in history lasted 180 hours," George said. "That's, like, seven and a half days!"

"I'll bet I can make a kite that flies higher and longer than you can," Manny told George.

"Bet you can't," George replied.

"It's a bet!" Manny agreed.

"I'll help you," Jeremy told Manny.

"With Jeremy helping, you'll definitely win," Becky assured Manny. She smiled brightly at Jeremy and batted her eyes.

Jeremy pretended not to hear Becky.

Katie took another bite of her sandwich and scowled. She hated it when kids from the two fourth-grade classes started bets. It always led to some sort of trouble.

But before Katie could do anything to stop the bet, Suzanne plopped down next to her. She was carrying an armload of magazines.

"These are my latest fashion magazines," Suzanne said to Katie. "There are some great hairstyles for you to look at."

"We're talking about kites, Suzanne," Jeremy told her.

"*You're* talking about kites," Suzanne said. "Katie and I have something much more important to discuss."

Katie sighed. She didn't feel like talking about hairstyles or kites. She felt like finishing the delicious peanut butter and banana sandwich her mother had packed for her.

But there was no stopping Suzanne. She had brought her magazines to school and she was going to make Katie look at them whether she wanted to or not.

"This one is pretty," Suzanne said, pointing to a photograph.

"That model has really long hair," Katie said. "My hair is too short to do that."

"You could *grow* it long," Suzanne suggested.

"Not by Monday night," Katie replied.

"That *is* pretty soon," Suzanne agreed. She pointed to another photo. "That hairstyle is cute."

Katie looked down at the picture. The model practically had a buzz cut.

"That's way too short,"

Katie said. "I like to put my hair in a ponytail sometimes."

Suzanne rolled her eyes. "Katie, to be stylish, you have to be daring," she said.

"Maybe, but I'm not going to be bald," Katie told Suzanne.

"Speaking of bald," George interrupted, "do you guys know what the bald man said when he got a comb for his birthday?"

"What?" Kevin asked.

"He said, 'I'll never part with it!'" George began to laugh at his own joke.

Katie laughed, too. George could be so funny sometimes.

Unfortunately, Suzanne didn't think so. "That was a really dumb joke," she told him. "Hairstyles are serious business. They're not something to joke about!"

That made George laugh even harder. Which made Suzanne even madder.

Just then, Emma W. picked up her flute case. "Katie, we have to go to band practice," she said.

"Great!" Katie exclaimed. She picked up her clarinet case and leaped out of her seat.

"Where are you going?" Suzanne demanded. "We still have a lot of hairstyles to look at. You can't leave now."

"She has to," Emma W. explained. "We're practicing during recess every day this week."

"But your hair . . ." Suzanne began.

"Sorry, Suzanne," Katie said. "I have to go. If the band doesn't practice, we won't be able to play in the concert. And then there won't be any reason for me to get a new hairstyle."

Suzanne couldn't argue with logic like that. "Okay, go ahead," she said. "But right after school, you and I are looking at these magazines. Every single one of them. We'll find you the perfect hairdo. You'll see."

Katie sighed as she looked at the huge stack of magazines on the table. Somehow Suzanne was turning the search for Katie's new 'do into a major *don't*!

Chapter 6

"Katie, sit still!" Suzanne insisted. "I can't get the rubber band around your hair if you move like that."

"Ouch!" Katie shouted as Suzanne tugged hard on her hair. "I don't know why we're doing this, anyway."

"We have to try things out so I know exactly what to tell Sparkle when we get to her salon," Suzanne explained.

Katie frowned. Why had she agreed to go to Suzanne's house after school? She should be practicing her clarinet instead. But there was something about Suzanne that made it impossible to say no. So for the past hour, Katie

had been sitting in Suzanne's bedroom, having her hair yanked, combed, tied, and curled.

"Ouch!" Katie cried out again. "What are you doing now?"

"I'm teasing," Suzanne said.

"What do you mean? What are you teasing me about?" Katie asked.

Suzanne giggled. "No, I meant, I'm teasing your *hair*," she explained. "I'm holding it at the ends and then combing it up instead of down. Teasing makes your hair more poofy."

"Why would I want poofy hair?" Katie asked.

"It will look absolutely great," Suzanne assured her. "Trust me."

Katie sighed. "If it looks so great, why won't you let me look in the mirror?" she wondered.

"Don't you want to be surprised?" Suzanne asked.

No. Katie did *not* want to be surprised. What she wanted was to go home.

"You're going to look so amazing! All the other moms and dads will be looking at you instead of their own kids," Suzanne continued.

Katie frowned. She didn't care about other parents. She just wanted her own dad to be there. But he was leaving tomorrow on his trip and wouldn't be home until Tuesday.

"Ouch!" Katie exclaimed as Suzanne tugged hard on a strand of her hair.

"Almost finished," Suzanne assured her. "Just another ribbon on the other side."

Just then, Suzanne's two-year-old sister, Heather, toddled into the room. She looked up at Katie and burst out laughing.

"Katie, you look silly," she said.

Suzanne glared at her little sister. "She does not," she told Heather. "Katie looks beautiful."

Heather shook her head. "Silly," she insisted. "Silly, silly, silly!"

"Mom!" Suzanne shouted at the top of her lungs. "Heather is ruining our playdate!"

Mrs. Lock came rushing down the hall. She bent down and scooped up Heather. Then she stared at Katie.

"What are you girls doing?" Mrs. Lock asked.

"We're trying out new hairstyles," Suzanne said proudly. "Don't you love what I've created for Katie?"

Mrs. Lock didn't say anything. She just kept staring at Katie's head.

"Mom?" Suzanne asked. "Didn't you hear me?"

"I heard you," Mrs. Lock replied. "I just don't know what to say."

Uh-oh. That didn't sound good. Katie leaped up out of the chair and dashed toward Suzanne's bedroom mirror.

"Aaaahhhh!" Katie screamed when she saw her reflection.

"What's wrong?" Suzanne asked. "I think it's perfect."

Katie stared at the wild, red nest of hair on the top of her head. Below were four messy braids sticking almost straight out. She started to scream again.

"I look like the Bride of Frankenstein!" Katie exclaimed.

"Don't worry, Katie," Mrs. Lock said. "As soon as you unbraid and brush your hair, it will go right back to normal."

"But I can't go home like this," Katie said.

"What if someone sees me?"

"I'll fix it now," Mrs. Lock assured her.

"Thanks," Katie said, choking back her
tears.

"You're going to change it back after all
my hard work?" Suzanne shouted angrily.
"That's the last time I'll try to make you look
gorgeous!"

Katie certainly hoped so.

Chapter 7

The next morning, Katie had pushed all thoughts of hair out of her head. She couldn't help feeling really sad when she kissed her dad good-bye.

"I feel just as bad as you do about missing the concert," Katie's father told her.

Katie knew he meant it. But it didn't make her feel any better. And to make things worse, Katie was really tired. She'd spent most of last night reading a book about things that glided, like flying squirrels, hang gliders, and, of course, kites. Katie couldn't wait to tell Mr. G. all the new things she'd learned.

Of course, Katie wasn't the only fourth-grader

thinking about how kites flew.

"I think we need more than one tail," she overheard Jeremy saying as she walked over to where he and Manny were standing on the playground. "That will keep the kite more stable when it's flying."

"Hi, guys," Katie greeted the boys cheerfully.

Manny frowned when he saw Katie.

"Hey, did you hear what Jeremy was saying?" he demanded.

"About what?" Katie wondered.

"About our kite," Manny said.

"I'm not sure," Katie admitted. "I think you said something about its tail."

"Oh, great," Manny said angrily. "Now the enemy will find out what we're planning."

"What *enemy*?" Katie asked. She was confused.

"George, Kadeem, and Kevin," Jeremy said.

"I bet you're on their side," Manny added.

"Why would I be on their side?" Katie asked.

"Because they're in your class," Manny replied.

"I don't want to choose a side," she said. And she meant it. After all, George, Kadeem, and Kevin were in Katie's class. But she and Jeremy had been friends since they were babies.

"You have to," Manny told her. "If you're not with us, then you're against us."

Katie sighed. This kite-flying thing had turned into more than just a friendly competition. It was a major kite fight!

* * *

Things got worse after lunch, when the kids in the beginning band went to rehearsal.

Katie sat down in her assigned seat—the third chair from the left. Emma W. sat down in her seat in the middle of the second row.

A moment later, Jeremy came into the room. Katie smiled up at him. But Jeremy pretended not to see her. He sat down behind his drums without saying a word.

Then Becky came into the band room. She had her big French horn with her. "Hi, Jeremy," she cooed as she took her place in the third row.

"Hi, Becky," Jeremy replied.

Now, that was weird. Talking to Becky but *not* talking to Katie—did Jeremy consider Katie the enemy now?

Before Katie could ask him, George and Kevin strolled into the band room together. George sat down at the keyboards. Kevin took his assigned seat on the left side of the room.

"Hi, Katie Kazoo," George greeted her. "Ready to play 'Go Tell Aunt Rhodie'?"

"Definitely," Katie told him. "I practiced it last night."

"I practiced, too," Kevin said.

"You guys are going to sound great," Mr. Starkey assured them.

Kadeem and Manny walked into the band room at almost the same time as Mr. Starkey. Kadeem sat down in his seat in the back row. Manny plopped down in the chair next to Kevin.

Kevin leaped out of his chair!

"What's the matter?" Mr. Starkey asked Kevin.

"I don't want to sit next to Manny anymore," Kevin explained.

"You have to sit next to him," Mr. Starkey said. "You both play the trumpet. The trumpets sit together in one section."

"Can't I sit next to Kadeem?" Kevin asked. "He's on the same team as I am. The class 4A kite-flying team."

"I'll sit next to you, Kevin," Emma W. said. "I'm on class 4A's team."

"Everyone stay right where you are," Mr. Starkey told the kids. "There are no teams in this music room. Music sounds best when we all work together."

Just then, Suzanne appeared in the doorway. Yikes! She was holding another fashion magazine with her finger stuck between the pages.

"What are you doing here?" Kadeem asked her. "You're not in the band."

"I know," Suzanne said. "I just stopped by to show Katie a hairstyle. We're both getting our haircut on Saturday morning."

"Saturday is three days away," George reminded Suzanne.

"Suzanne, please leave at once. We are trying to have a rehearsal," Mr. Starkey said.

"Sorry," Suzanne said, although she didn't really sound very sorry. "These appointments are very, very important. Sparkle is only fitting Katie in as a favor to me."

Katie didn't really believe that. After all, Sparkle's Salon was brand-new. Sparkle needed as many customers as she could get. But Katie didn't say that to Suzanne. She didn't want to embarrass her in front of everyone.

So instead she said, "I'll see you later, Suzanne."

"Great," Suzanne said. "I'll meet you after school. I have some awesome pictures for you to look at. Have you ever considered getting a Mohawk?"

Katie didn't even know how to answer that one.

As Suzanne left the band room, Katie tried to concentrate on the songs she was about to play. But it was hard to think about "Camptown Races" when everyone else was fighting. If the kids in the beginning band didn't start to work together, they were going to sound terrible at the concert. How embarrassing would that be?

Katie frowned. This was *soooo* not good.

Chapter 8

And things didn't get any better as the week went on. By Friday, the fighting in the fourth grade was totally out of control. No one in class 4A was speaking to anyone in class 4B. Well, except for Suzanne. She was still talking to Katie.

Or rather, she was telling Katie what to do. *Constantly.*

"I don't think you should wear your hair super-straight," Suzanne said as the girls walked through the mall together on Saturday morning. "It would be too much work to straighten it every day."

"I'm just going to ask Sparkle what she

thinks I should do," Katie said. "After all, she's the professional."

Suzanne's face turned all red and angry. "*I'm a professional*," she insisted. "I've modeled three times."

"But those were recitals for your modeling class," Katie reminded her.

"I told you, they're not recitals. They're called *runway shows*," Suzanne insisted.

Katie rolled her eyes and sighed.

"Hey, isn't that George, Kevin, and Kadeem?" Suzanne said, pointing straight ahead. "What are they doing here? They don't need haircuts."

"There are lots of stores in the mall, Suzanne," Katie reminded her friend.

"I guess," Suzanne agreed. "I'm just so focused on our haircuts, I can't think about anything else."

That made Katie laugh. What a Suzanne thing to say.

"Hi, Katie Kazoo," George greeted her a

moment later. He didn't say anything to Suzanne. After all, she was in class 4B. *The enemy.*

"You guys have been doing a lot of shopping," Katie said, pointing to three huge bags they were carrying.

"We're buying supplies for—" Kevin began.

Kadeem poked Kevin in the side and pointed to Suzanne.

"We're just buying stuff," Kevin murmured.

"*We're* off to get haircuts," Suzanne told the boys. "And we're late already."

Suzanne grabbed Katie by the arm and started to pull her away. Katie lost her balance. She grabbed at George to keep from tripping. Instead she grabbed his shopping bag and it ripped.

Everything spilled out of George's bag. There were bright red pom-poms, a bag of big, plastic googly eyes, and a long, green and purple ribbon.

George glared at Suzanne. "You did that on purpose!" he insisted. "You were trying to make Katie fall!"

Suzanne shot him a look. "And just why would I want to do that?"

"Because you're a spy!" George told her. "You wanted to see our kite materials."

"You're using googly eyes for your kite?" Katie asked George.

"I don't want to talk about it in front of *her*," George told Katie.

Suzanne rolled her eyes. "I couldn't care less about your stupid kite." And with that, Suzanne stormed off in the direction of Sparkle's Salon.

"I'm sorry," Katie told the boys. She bent down and picked up the pom-poms and the ribbon.

"Be careful around her, Katie Kazoo," George warned. "Remember, she's the enemy."

Katie's mind raced back to the weird hairdo Suzanne had created for her earlier in the week. A nervous feeling came over her. Could George be right?

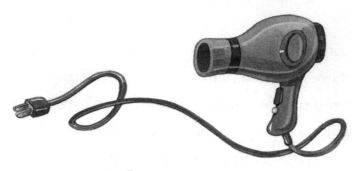

Chapter 9

A moment later, Katie walked into Sparkle's Salon. Wow! This place definitely did not look like any hair salon Katie had ever been to before.

"This is amazing!" Suzanne exclaimed. "I love it."

Katie could understand why. Suzanne loved glitter. And walking into Sparkle's Salon was like entering a glitter factory—where there had been an explosion! There was glitter and sparkles everywhere. Sparkly stars were painted on the ceiling. A glittery rainbow covered the entire back wall.

But nothing in the salon was as sparkly as

Sparkle herself! She was wearing a shimmery gold dress, which matched her gold, glitter-covered platform shoes. Her hot pink hair and long, blue nails were covered with glitter, too.

"Wow!" Suzanne exclaimed. "Sparkle looks so cool. I'd love to have an outfit just like that."

Katie could definitely see Suzanne in a gold sparkly dress. But she couldn't see herself in one. She couldn't see herself with hot pink hair, either.

"I don't know about this, Suzanne," Katie said slowly.

"What are you talking about?" Suzanne asked her. "Sparkle has such a sense of style."

"Not *my* style," Katie insisted. "I don't want weird-colored hair."

Katie turned around to head for the door. That was when she saw that Sparkle was standing right behind her. There was no way Sparkle could have missed hearing what Katie had just said. That made Katie feel awful. She hadn't meant to hurt Sparkle's

feelings. Pink hair looked just fine on Sparkle. Katie just didn't want it for herself.

But Sparkle didn't seem angry with Katie. In fact, she smiled at her.

"Hello, girls," Sparkle said. "Do you have appointments?"

"We sure do!" Suzanne said. "Both of us."

Katie gulped. She couldn't leave now. That

would be rude. Katie was trapped.

"I'm Suzanne, and this is my friend Katie," Suzanne explained.

Sparkle smiled again. "It's a pleasure to meet you both."

Katie nodded. "Um . . . hi," she said, trying not to stare at the glittery blue lip gloss Sparkle was wearing.

"So who wants to go first?" Sparkle asked.

Without thinking, Katie pushed her best friend in front of her. "Suzanne does," she said quickly. "I can wait."

Sparkle shrugged and said, "Okay, however you girls want it. Go into the dressing rooms and put on smocks. I'll be right with you."

As she watched Suzanne walk into a dressing room, Katie thought about making a run for it. But she knew she couldn't.

Katie shut the door behind her in one of the other dressing rooms. She stood there for a minute, looking into the long, full-length mirror. It felt really strange knowing that this might be the last time she ever saw herself looking like this. Normal.

Just then, Katie felt a cool wind blowing on the back of her neck. That was weird. There were no windows in the dressing room. And no fans, either.

Where was the breeze coming from?

The wind began blowing colder and harder, then whirring around until it was like a wild tornado. *A tornado that was only spinning around Katie.*

Oh no! This wasn't an ordinary wind. It was the magic wind. And, boy, was it blowing. The wind was so fierce, Katie was afraid it might blow her right out of the mall. Maybe even all the way out of Cherrydale!

Katie shut her eyes tight and tried not to cry.

And then it stopped. Just like that. The magic wind was gone.

So was Katie Kazoo. She'd been turned into someone else. One, two, switcheroo!

But who?

Chapter 10

"I want something that will stand out when I walk down the runway. I want to be the model everybody remembers."

Katie knew that was Suzanne talking, even before she opened her eyes. She would recognize her best friend's voice anywhere.

But of course she hadn't gone *anywhere*. If Suzanne was talking, then Katie was still in Sparkle's Salon. So now Katie knew where she was. But she still didn't know *who* she was.

Slowly, Katie opened her eyes. She looked down. Instead of seeing her red high-top sneakers, Katie's eyes fell on a pair of glittery gold platform shoes.

Katie looked at her hands. Her nails were painted blue. And she was holding a pair of scissors.

That could only mean one thing! The magic wind had switcherooed Katie into Sparkle, *right before Suzanne's haircut!*

At the moment, Suzanne was standing in a gold glittery robe in the middle of the salon. She was smiling broadly. Katie sighed. Suzanne wouldn't be so happy if she knew who her new stylist really was!

Once, Katie had gotten gum in her hair and tried to cut it out herself. That was all she knew about cutting hair. And it had been a big mistake. If Suzanne didn't like her hairstyle, she was going to get very, very mad. Katie had to find some way to get out of cutting Suzanne's hair. She just had to!

"You know, Suzanne," Katie said quickly. "I don't think you need a haircut. Your hair looks pretty spectacular the way it is."

Suzanne smiled. "I know," she agreed. "But

pretty spectacular isn't good enough for this runway show. I want my hair to look *incredibly* spectacular!"

Katie sighed again. Once Suzanne decided on something, there was no way to stop her. Katie was going to have to cut Suzanne's hair.

"Um, okay," Katie said slowly.

"So what are you going to do?" Suzanne asked.

"It's going to be a surprise," Katie said. *To both of us,* she thought.

Katie held the scissors in the air and looked at Suzanne's head. She had no idea where to start.

At just that moment the salon door opened and two women came in. Katie gulped. They must have appointments with Sparkle, too.

"You're way too early," Katie told them. "Why don't you go home?"

The women looked at Katie oddly.

"That's okay," one of them said. "We don't mind waiting. It will be fun to see what you do with this girl's hair."

Katie frowned as the two women sat down. Oh,

great. Now she had an audience.

Suzanne sat there, looking in the mirror at both her reflection and Katie's.

"Don't look in the mirror!" Katie insisted nervously. "I can't cut your hair if you're staring at me."

Suzanne looked puzzled. "Why not?" she asked.

"I . . . I just . . . um . . . I want you to be surprised," Katie stammered. She turned Suzanne's chair around so she couldn't see the mirror anymore.

"But I want to see," Suzanne insisted.

"I wanted to see, too, but you wouldn't let me, remember?" Katie reminded her.

"What are you talking about?" Suzanne sounded really confused.

Oops. No wonder Suzanne was confused. She didn't know that it was her best friend who was cutting her hair. Suzanne thought Katie was Sparkle.

"I mean, I never let any of my really special

clients see my work before it's done," Katie explained. "I like them to be surprised."

"Oh, okay," Suzanne said with a smile. She obviously liked being called a "really special client."

Phew. That was a close one.

Slowly, Katie held up the scissors. She made a snip here and a cut there. Then a snip at the bottom. And a cut near the top.

Snip. Cut. Snip. Cut.

Katie smiled. The two women watching weren't making faces. Maybe this wasn't as hard as she thought it would be. And Suzanne's hair didn't look bad. Not at all.

Chapter 11

At least, it didn't look bad to Katie. Suzanne, on the other hand, had a very different reaction.

"Aaaaahhhh!" she shouted the second Katie spun her chair around so she could look in the mirror. "What have you done to me?"

"Don't you like it?" Katie asked her.

"Like it? I hate it!" Suzanne exclaimed. "The left side is longer than the right side. The bangs are all choppy, and there are these two pieces sticking out over my right ear."

Katie studied Suzanne's head. Funny, she hadn't noticed any of those things before.

At first, neither of the other customers said

a word. The women just stood there with their mouths open. But then, they began talking at once.

"I . . . um . . . I just remembered. I have to feed my cat," one woman said after catching a glimpse of Suzanne's zigzagging bangs. She ran out of the shop.

"And I . . . well . . . I have to go home and . . . um . . . wash my hair," the other customer added nervously.

"But you're in a *hair salon*," Katie reminded her. She pointed to the sinks in the back of the shop. "Sparkle . . . I mean . . . *I* can wash it here."

The woman didn't answer. She just headed for the door.

Now Katie and Suzanne were the only ones left in the shop. At least for the moment.

"My mother is going to be here any minute," Suzanne shouted. "She's going to go bonkers."

"Suzanne, please, be quiet," Katie pleaded with her. "Sparkle's . . . I mean, *I'm* losing all my customers."

"I don't care!" Suzanne exclaimed loudly.

Katie couldn't believe how mean her friend was being. Katie had tried her best to give her a good haircut. Hair cutting was really hard. But Suzanne didn't care about that. All she cared about was herself.

Suddenly Katie felt tears building up in her eyes. But she couldn't let Suzanne see her cry. Katie was pretty sure real hairstylists never cried. "Ex-excuse me," Katie stammered unhappily. "I . . . um . . . I have to go find some extra-strength hair spray to hold your hair in place."

"I don't want my hair to stay this way!" Suzanne shouted.

Katie barely heard her. She was already on

her way to a supply closet that was in the back of the salon.

Katie's tears started to fall the minute the door slammed behind her. She felt terrible about everything that happened.

As Katie thought about Suzanne's uneven hair and the customers who had run out of the store, she felt a cool breeze on the back of her neck. She looked around. There were no windows in the closet. And no fans, either. And yet the breeze kept blowing. But only around Katie.

That could only mean one thing. This was no ordinary wind. This was the magic wind!

The magic wind grew stronger and stronger, circling around Katie like a wild tornado. It almost knocked her off her platform shoes. Katie shut her eyes tight.

And then it stopped. Just like that. The magic wind was gone. Katie Kazoo was back!

So was Sparkle. And boy, was she confused!

"Wh-where am I?" Sparkle asked, shaking her

head slightly and looking around.

"You're in your supply closet," Katie replied. "Don't you recognize it?"

"I do," Sparkle said. "But why am I in here?"

"You needed to get away from Suzanne," Katie explained. "She was mad, and she was screaming, and I—I mean, *you*—couldn't take it anymore, so you ran off. You said you were looking for hair spray."

"Why was Suzanne mad?" Sparkle asked Katie.

"The haircut wasn't what she wanted," Katie said.

"The haircut?" Sparkle asked. She was totally confused. "I cut Suzanne's hair?"

Before Katie could say another word, she heard a loud voice coming from outside the supply closet.

"Where is she?" a woman demanded. "Where's Sparkle?"

Katie knew that voice. "That's Suzanne's mom," she told Sparkle.

"I'd better go talk to her," Sparkle said. "Although I'm not sure what I'm going to say."

"There's the person who ruined my hair! There she is!" Suzanne shouted as Sparkle and Katie came out of the supply closet.

"I didn't ruin anything!" Katie shouted.

Suzanne stared at Katie. "Not you," she said. "Sparkle."

Oops. "I meant your hair's not ruined," Katie said.

"Yes, it is," Suzanne said. "And my modeling show is in two hours. I don't have time to get it fixed."

"Of course you do," Sparkle said. "I can fix anything. Just sit back down in the chair and—"

"I think you've done quite enough," Mrs. Lock said. "We're leaving." She took Suzanne by the hand. Then she turned to Katie. "Aren't you coming?"

Katie looked around. The salon was empty. Katie felt awful. After all, this was her fault.

She had to do something to make Sparkle feel better.

"No," Katie told Mrs. Lock. "I need a haircut. My mom is working at the bookstore. She'll come by and pay for my cut when Sparkle is finished."

"Katie, you're nuts," Suzanne said. "You could wind up looking like a witch."

Katie shook her head. "I'm sure I'll look just fine." Katie sat down in the salon chair and swallowed hard. "Okay, Sparkle. Let's get started," she assured the stylist.

But she wasn't really so sure. Sparkle was kind of a weird lady. What if she did something weird to Katie's hair—something even weirder than what Katie had done to Suzanne's?

Chapter 12

Sparkle was like a magician with scissors. She gave Katie a trim and added some cool, new, layered bangs. At first, Katie felt a little sad that her dad wouldn't be at the concert and would have to wait to see her new hairstyle. But by the time she arrived at Suzanne's modeling school to see her runway show, Katie was in a good mood.

"Oh, Katie, there you are!" Mrs. Lock exclaimed. "You have to make Suzanne change her mind!"

"About what?" Katie asked.

"She's refusing to go on because of her hair," Mrs. Lock said. "I've tried talking to her, but it's no use."

Katie wasn't sure what she could say that would make Suzanne feel any better. But she knew she had to try.

"Where is she?" Katie asked.

"Backstage," Mrs. Lock said. "You can't miss her."

⭐ ⭐ ⭐

That was the truth. There were at least twenty girls backstage, but Suzanne was the only one with a brown paper bag on her head. She was also the only one crying.

"Hi, Suzanne," Katie greeted her.

"Hi, Katie," Suzanne said between sobs.

"Are you almost ready?" Katie asked. "You go on in a few minutes."

"Oh no!" Suzanne said. "I'm not going on. I can't let anyone see me."

Katie sighed. "Yeah. You're right," she said finally.

"I am?" Suzanne asked. She sounded surprised.

Katie nodded. "It's not like you're a real model or this is a real runway show or anything."

"I am a real model!" Suzanne declared. She took the paper bag off her head.

"No, you're not," Katie said. "A real model would go on no matter what. She would make it work. But you . . ."

"I can make this work. I can make anything work." Suzanne picked up a comb and started smoothing down her hair. "You'd better leave, Katie. I have only a couple of minutes before my big moment!"

★ ★ ★

"I don't know what you said to Suzanne," Mrs. Lock told Katie after the runway show. "But it worked. She looked great up there."

"I know," Katie agreed.

"Oh! There she is," Mrs. Lock exclaimed. She scooped up Heather and hurried over to Suzanne. Katie followed close behind.

A large crowd of modeling students had gathered around Suzanne. Some were about the same age as Suzanne and Katie. Some of them looked like teenagers. But they were all talking about the same thing—Suzanne's hair!

"I love your asymmetrical cut," one of the teenagers said to Suzanne.

"My *what* cut?" Suzanne asked her.

"Asymmetrical," the girl said. "It means when the sides aren't even. It's the newest thing. I saw it in a magazine."

"Oh," Suzanne said. "Of course. I made a special request when I went to the salon. I said exactly what I wanted."

Katie choked back a laugh. That wasn't quite the way it had happened.

"What salon?" another teenage girl asked.

"Sparkle's Salon," Suzanne said. "In the mall. It's brand-new. I *discovered* it."

The teenage girls pulled out their cell phones. "I'm calling her right now!" one of them declared.

"I'm definitely going to that salon," another teen agreed.

"Sparkle is clearly a genius," her friend added.

"Sparkle's not the genius," Suzanne insisted. "I am. *I'm* the one who asked her for something that would make me stand out."

But the teenage girls weren't listening to Suzanne anymore. They were too busy calling for appointments at Sparkle's Salon.

Katie walked over and smiled at Suzanne. "You were a hit."

Suzanne nodded. "I know," she said. "But they're all thinking it was Sparkle who came up with this haircut. And it wasn't Sparkle who did it at all."

Katie laughed. Suzanne had no idea just how true that statement really was. And she never would. The magic wind was Katie's secret.

Chapter 13

Katie was definitely glad when Monday rolled around. It had been kind of a lonely weekend without her dad home. They always made breakfast together on Sunday mornings while Katie's mom slept late. But not this Sunday. And Katie had to watch the baseball game on TV by herself. The Cherrydale Porcupines had really whipped the Surreytown Tigers. But no one was around for Katie to cheer with.

There would be plenty of cheering today, though. The boys were all set for their kite-flying contest. Katie didn't care whose kite could fly higher and longer. She just wanted all the arguing and secret keeping to be over.

"You better wrap your kite in a trash bag," Manny told George, Kadeem, and Kevin. "Our kite is going to make yours look like garbage."

"No way!" Kadeem shouted. "Our kite rocks!"

"Meet the clown kite," George said. He held their kite up for everyone to see.

Katie giggled. The kite was funny. The boys had decorated it with a red pom-pom clown nose and big googly eyes. The tail was a long green and purple ribbon.

Jeremy and Manny's kite was smaller. It was decorated with superhero stickers, and it had two tails made from long red, white, and blue ribbons.

"Are you ready to fly your kite?" Jeremy asked the boys from 4A.

"The *real* question is, are you ready to lose the kite fight?" George asked Jeremy.

"We're not going to lose," Jeremy said confidently.

"Stop the arguing, dudes," Mr. G. told the

kids. "Let's get these kites in the air."

"Are you all ready?" Ms. Sweet asked Jeremy, Manny, Kadeem, George, and Kevin

The boys nodded.

"Good," Ms. Sweet said with a smile. "Then let the kite flying begin!"

The boys didn't have to be told twice. Jeremy took off running with the superhero kite while Manny held the string. Almost immediately, the superhero kite took flight.

At the same time, Kadeem ran with the clown kite while George unrolled the string. Kadeem let go. The clown kite flew into the air.

"Ours is higher!" Kadeem shouted excitedly.

"No way," Manny shouted. He loosened a little more string so the superhero kite could fly higher.

George unrolled more string, too. The clown kite flew higher, too.

Katie looked up and watched as the kites moved back and forth in the wind. They drifted closer to each other until . . .

Suddenly their strings got all tangled up. Both kites fell to the ground!

"Oh no!" Jeremy cried out.

"You did that on purpose," George told Manny and Jeremy.

"We did not," Manny said. "You flew your kite too close to ours," he told George, Kadeem, and Kevin.

"It doesn't matter whose fault it is," Kevin said with a frown. "We can't fly our kites anymore."

"Yes, you can," Suzanne piped up.

The kids all turned around to look at her.

"All you have to do is untangle the strings

and start over," she said.

"But they're just going to get all tangled again," Jeremy told her.

Suzanne shook her head. "You just have to do this like a fashion show."

"A kite fashion show?" George asked her. "There's no such thing."

Suzanne rolled her eyes. "I didn't mean you were modeling kites, George," she explained. "I just meant that in a fashion show, everyone takes a turn walking down the runway. When one person finishes, the next one goes."

"You mean take turns," Manny said.

Suzanne nodded. "Exactly."

"Why didn't you just say that?" Kevin asked.

"Because then it wouldn't have been a *Suzanne* idea," Katie told the boys.

The kids all laughed. That was true. Suzanne definitely had her own way of saying things.

"How will we know who wins the contest if the kites don't fly at the same time?" Manny asked.

"Dudes, you're all winners," Mr. G. assured the boys. "You made kites that are designed to fly high for a long time."

"Yeah, that's true," Jeremy said.

"We're the kings of kites," George agreed with a smile.

"Okay, Your Highness," Katie said with a giggle. "Let's see your kite take flight!"

★ ★ ★

A few minutes later, the clown kite was flying

high in the air. Jeremy and Manny were waiting nearby for their turn to fly the superhero kite.

Suddenly Katie felt a cool breeze blowing on the back of her neck. *Oh no,* she thought. *Not the magic wind. Not now!*

But as she looked around, Katie could see that the leaves were blowing in the breeze. And some of the kids had buttoned their jackets.

Phew. It was just a regular old wind. The kind of wind that made kites fly. And that kind of wind made Katie Kazoo very, very happy.

Chapter 14

Go tell Aunt Rhodie. Go tell Aunt Rhodie. Go tell Aunt Rhodie. The old gray goose is dead.

The audience cheered as the beginning band finished the song. Katie tried to look out into the audience to see her mom and Suzanne, but the stage lights were so bright, she couldn't see anyone.

When the concert ended, Katie raced into the audience. She was excited to hear what her mom and Suzanne thought about the beginning band.

But when Katie got to where her mom was sitting, she got a big surprise!

"Daddy!" she shouted. "You're here!"

Katie's dad grinned. "I couldn't miss my Kit Kat's first concert. I was able to get an early flight home."

"I wanted it to be a surprise," her mom added.

Katie gave her dad a huge hug. "This is the best surprise!" she told her parents.

"Hey, what about me?" Suzanne asked. "I came to see you, too."

"Thank you," Katie replied. "Did you like the concert?"

"It was great," Suzanne said. "And you looked really nice up there. But I still think you should have gotten a whole new hairstyle. Just like I did."

Katie looked at Suzanne. Her hair was amazing. She'd gone back to Sparkle to have her fix it up. Sparkle's version of the haircut was a lot better than Katie's had been.

"I think you're both beautiful," Katie's father said. "How about I take you gorgeous girls out for ice cream?"

Katie grinned. Ice cream! Yum! Now *that* was music to her ears!

About the Author

Nancy Krulik is the author of more than 150 books for children and young adults, including three *New York Times* best sellers. She lives in New York City with her husband, composer Daniel Burwasser, their children, Amanda and Ian, and Pepper, a chocolate and white spaniel mix. When she's not busy writing the Katie Kazoo, Switcheroo series, Nancy loves swimming, reading, and going to the movies.

About the Illustrators

John & Wendy have illustrated all of the Katie Kazoo books, but when they're not busy drawing Katie and her friends, they like to paint, take photographs, travel, and play music in their rock 'n' roll band. They live and work in Brooklyn, New York.